AUG - - 2015

W9-BTA-783

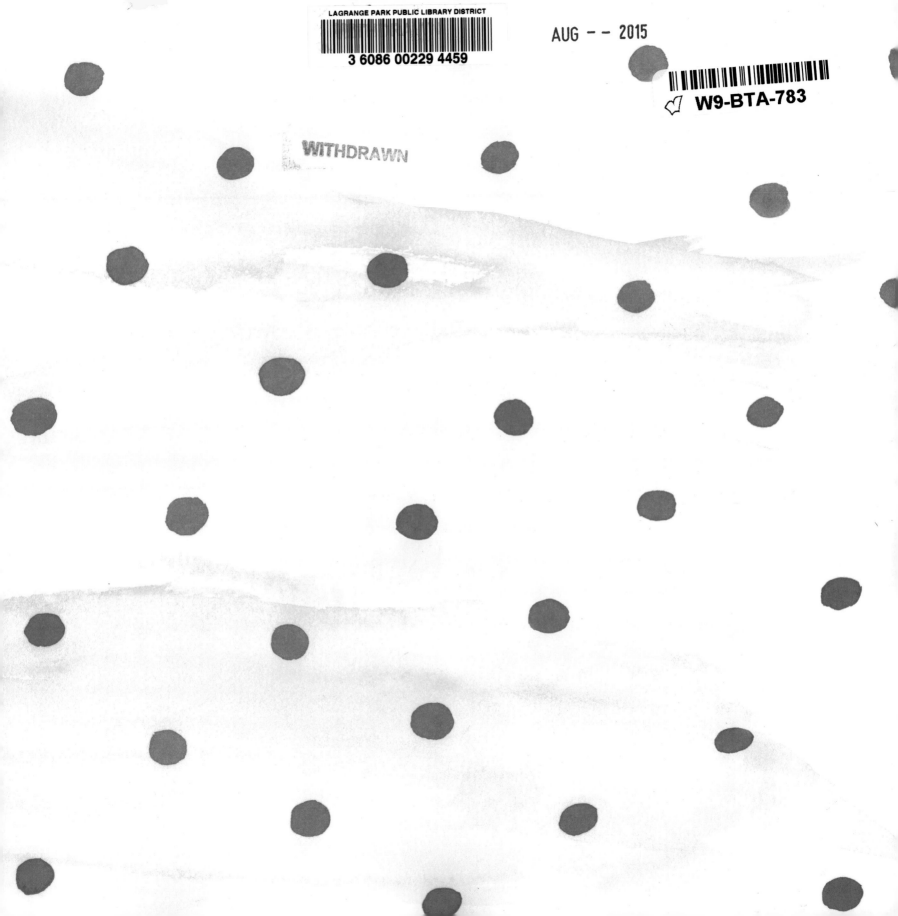

Little BIG

JONATHAN BENTLEY

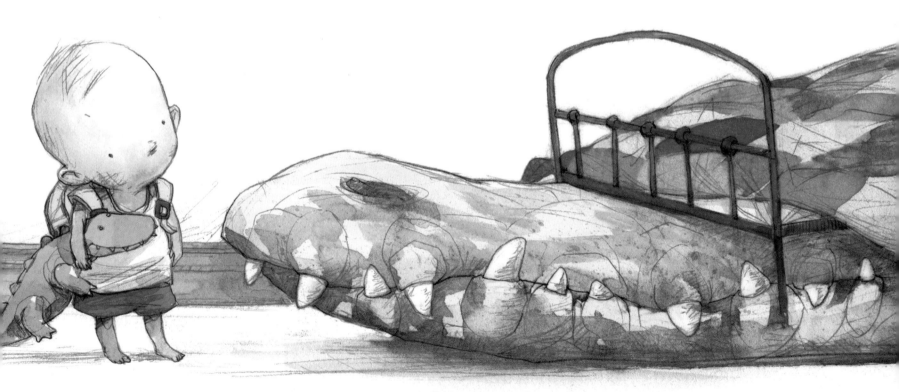

EERDMANS BOOKS FOR YOUNG READERS

GRAND RAPIDS, MICHIGAN • CAMBRIDGE, U.K.

I am little.

I try to be **big**.

But it never works.

Little.
Little legs,
little hands,
little mouth.

If I had **big legs** like a giraffe,
I could race my brother up the hill . . .
and win.

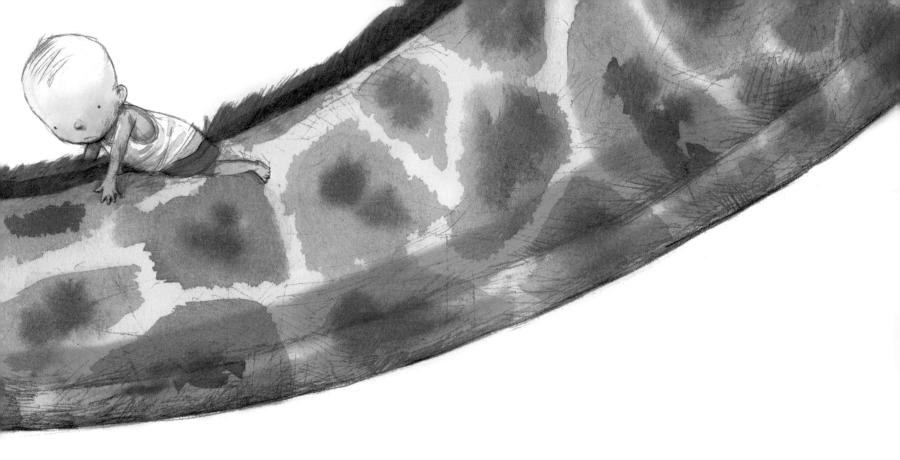

But I wouldn't be able to ride in the wagon.

If I had **big hands** like a gorilla,
I could open the cookie jar

and take as many cookies
as I wanted.

But I wouldn't be able to eat them in my playhouse.

If I had a **big mouth** like a crocodile,

I could tell my big brother
to go to bed early.

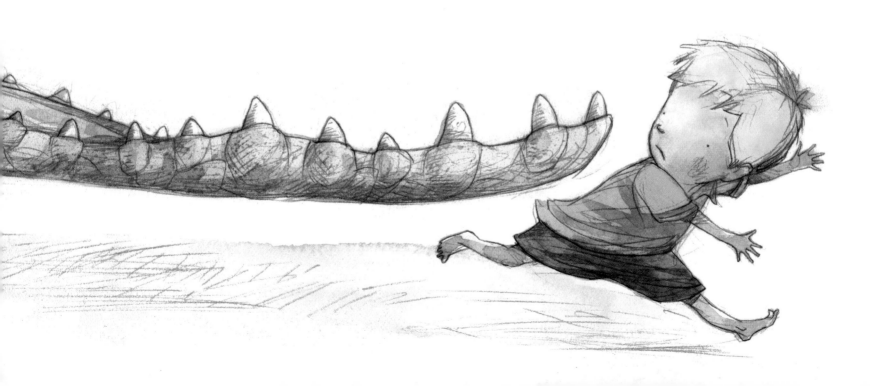

But who would tell me funny stories after dinner?

If I was **big** like a **monster**, I could . . .

Run, run, run, little legs.

Hold on tight, little hands.

Not a sound, little mouth.

I am little.

Little legs, little hands, little mouth.

Perfectly little.

For my family — J.B.

First published in the United States in 2015 by
Eerdmans Books for Young Readers,
an imprint of Wm. B. Eerdmans Publishing Co.
2140 Oak Industrial Dr. NE
Grand Rapids, Michigan 49505
P.O. Box 163, Cambridge CB3 9PU U.K.

www.eerdmans.com/youngreaders

Originally published in Australia in 2013
by Little Hare Books,
an imprint of Hardie Grant Egmont
Ground Floor, Building 1, 658 Church Street
Richmond, Victoria 3121, Australia
www.littleharebooks.com

Text and illustrations © 2013 Jonathan Bentley

15 16 17 18 19 20 21   9 8 7 6 5 4 3 2 1

Library of Congress Cataloging-in-Publication Data

Bentley, Jonathan, author, illustrator.
Little big / by Jonathan Bentley.
pages cm
Summary: A little boy imagines what it would be like to be big, with long legs
like a giraffe, big hands like a gorilla, or a big mouth like a crocodile,
but realizes that there are advantages to being perfectly little.
ISBN 978-0-8028-5462-9
[1. Size — Fiction. 2. Imagination — Fiction. 3. Brothers — Fiction.] I. Title.
PZ7.1.B4545Lit 2015
[E] — dc23
2014048096

The illustrations in this book were created using watercolors, pencil, and scanned textures.